The Cactus Dance
La Danza del Cactus

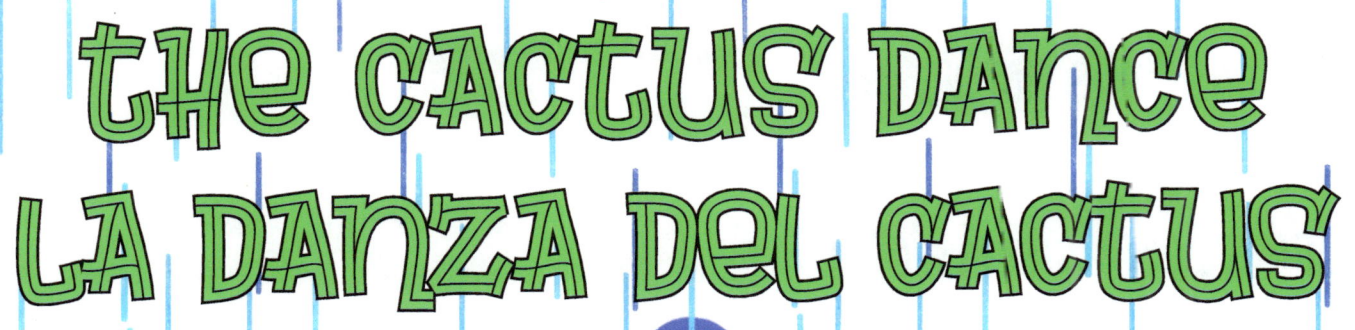

For Tim, Andrew, Jerome, & DJ

written by April Lesher

illustrated by Gabriela Vega

This edition first published in 2023
by Lawley Publishing,
a division of Lawley Enterprises LLC.

Text Copyright © 2023 by April Lesher
Illustration Copyright © 2023 by Gabriela Vega
All Rights Reserved

Hardcover ISBN 978-1-956357-93-6
Paperback ISBN 978-1-956357-95-0
Library of Congress Control Number: 2022934502

Lawley Publishing
70 S. Val Vista Dr. #A3 #188
Gilbert, AZ 85296
www.LawleyPublishing.com

Cactus lifts up his arms
Cactus levanta sus brazos
and sticks out his chin.
y saca su barbilla.

He whispers, "Aaaah, aaaah"
Susurra, "Aaaah, aaaah"
as the sun warms his skin.
mientras el sol calienta su piel.

He whistles and waves,
El silba y saluda,
relaxes and sways,
se relaja y balancea,

until a dribble, a drop,
hasta un hilillo, una gota,

a plink and a plop.
un tintin, un plaf.

and stomps his boots.
y zapatea sus botas.

Javelina growls,
 jabalí gruñe,

coyote howls,
coyote aúlla,

and the desert starts shouting, "Yippee!"
y el desierto comienza a gritar, "¡Yippeee!"

Cactus twirls his toes
Cactus remolinea los dedos de los pies

and wrinkles his nose.
y arruga la nariz.

Lizards swish,
Lagartijas se mueven,
rattlesnakes hiss,
culebras silban,

and the reptiles start calling, "Yippee!"
y los reptiles comienzan a gritar, "¡Yippee!"

Cactus shakes his spines,
Cactus sacude sus agujas,

and jiggles his lines.
y menea sus líneas.

until a dribble, a drop,
hasta un hilillo, un gota,

a plink and a plop,
un tintin, un plaf,

Cactus lifts up his arms
Cactus levanta sus brazos

and sticks out his chin.
y saca su barbilla.

He whispers, "Aaaah, aaaah"
Susurra, "Aaaah, aaaah"

as the sun dries his skin.
mientras el sol seca su piel.

April Lesher lives in Mesa, Arizona, where she enjoys the sunny days and the wild spirit of the Southwest. Most of her writing reflects her affinity for the culture and beauty of the 48th state. She earned her master's degree from Arizona State University and currently teaches in Gilbert. During monsoon season, April can be found splashing in the desert rain with her family and two dogs.

Gabriela Vega is a proud Latina children's book illustrator from California and a recent graduate from Cal State Fullerton, where she received her Bachelor of Fine Arts. Gabriela enjoys incorporating simple shapes, different textures, and bright colors in her work. She has won two awards from the Society of Children's Book Writers and Illustrators and was selected as a mentee for the 2022 WNDB Mentorship Program. Besides having a passion for illustration, Gabriela aspires to become an art teacher someday and will continue her education at Cal State San Bernardino.

CPSIA information can be obtained
at www.ICGtesting.com
Printed in the USA
BVHW062331031222
653399BV00004B/38